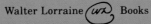

HOUGHTON MIFFLIN COMPANY BOSTON 2002

Walter Lorraine Books

For my mother

Walter Lorraine wr Books

Copyright © 2002 by Seymour Chwast

www.houghtonmifflinbooks.com

Library of Congress Cataloging-in-Publication Data

Chwast, Seymour.
    Harry, I need you! / by Seymour Chwast.
    p. cm.
    Summary: When Harry's mother calls him to get out of bed to see a surprise,
he tries to imagine what it could be.
    ISBN 0-618-17917-8
    [1. Imagination—Fiction. 2. Surprise—Fiction.] I. Chwast, Seymour, ill. II. Title.

PZ7.Z487 Haqp 2002
[E]—dc21   2001039416

Printed in China
HZI 10 9 8 7 6 5 4 3 2 1

Get out of
bed, Harry.
I'm waiting. . .

Maybe there's a robot at the door who wants to speak to me.

Maybe Goldilocks
and the three bears
came for breakfast.

Maybe a dinosaur
wants a glass of water.

Maybe
the oven
caught fire.

Maybe aliens want to use the telephone.

Maybe there's an earthquake and we have to get out of the house.

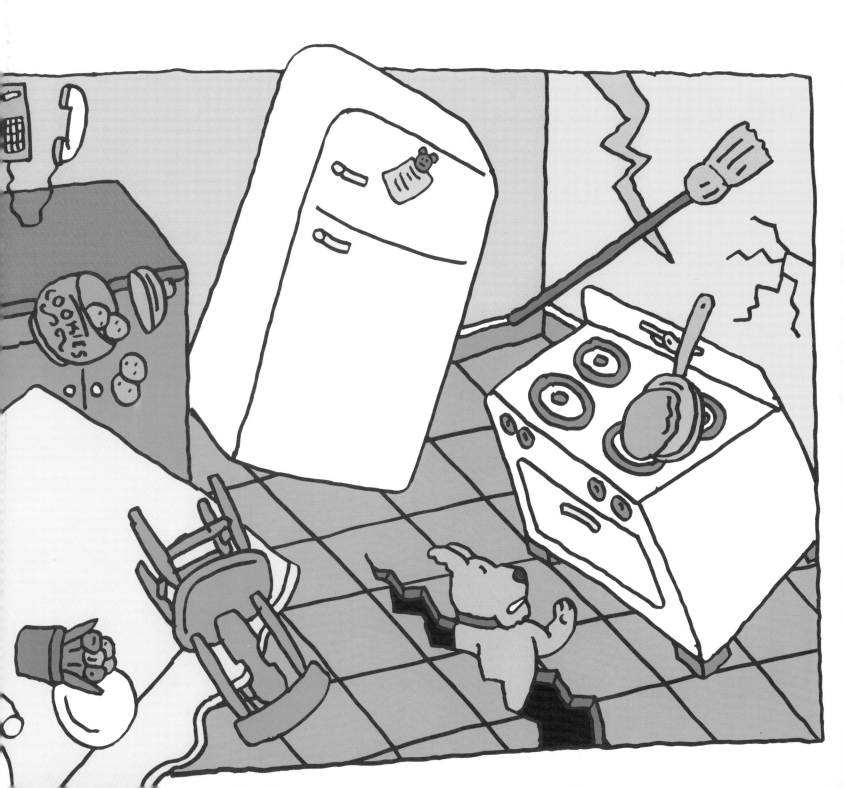

Maybe a robber stole cookies from the cookie jar.

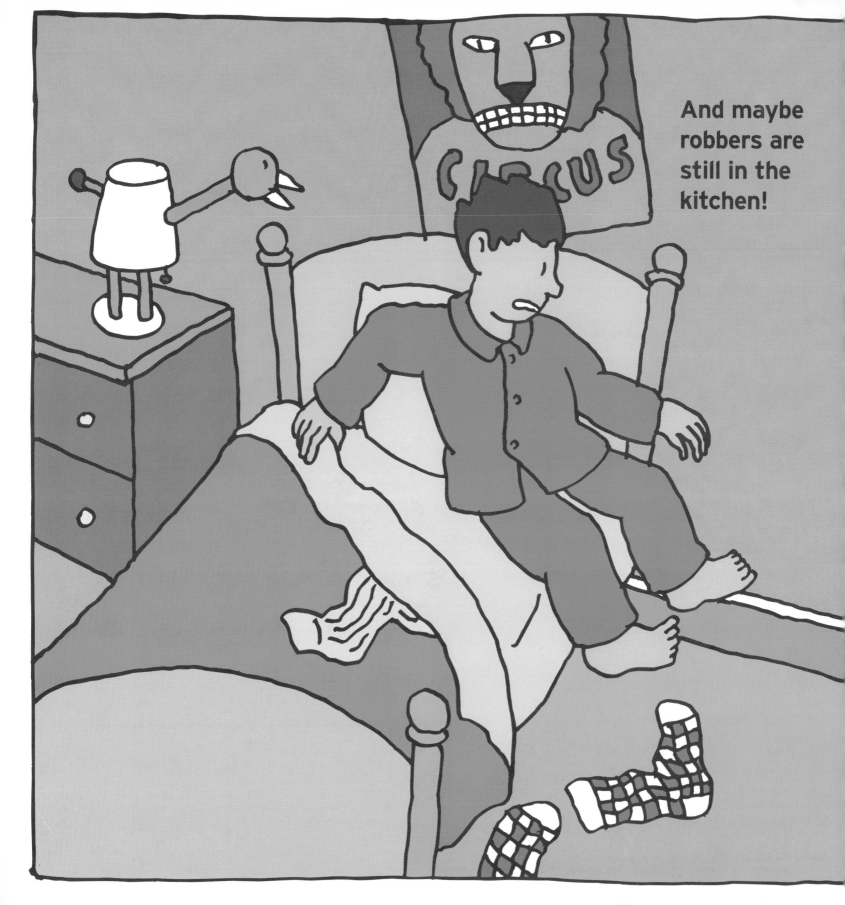

And maybe robbers are still in the kitchen!

What robbers? There are no robbers. But there's a big surprise in the back hall.